E
MI

Miller, Virginia
On your potty

$13.95

DATE			
OC 15 '91	SEP 21 '95	MY 05 '99	AP 07 '04
JA 27 '92	OCT 05 '95	MR 17 00	AG 26 '05
FE 6 '92	OCT 19 '95	FE 10 '01	JY 09 '08
JY 2 '92	NOV 15 '95	JY 24 01	JE 23 '10
JUL 23 '92	DEC 26 '95	NO 08 '00	JY 08 '16
DE 28 '92	MR 14 '96	JY 09 '02	
MR 6 '93	APR 09 '96	AG 05 02	
JY 8 '93	MAY 30 '96	MR 25 '03	
SE 5 '93	JUN 27 '96	JE 05 '03	
NOV 20 '93	APR 15 '97	JY 1 '03	
MAY 28 '94	APR 15 '99	JY 23 03	
AUG 08 '94	29 '99	JY 08 '04	

© THE BAKER & TAYLOR CO.

**For Swee Hong
and James**

VIRGINIA MILLER

ON YOUR POTTY!

 GREENWILLOW BOOKS, New York

Copyright © 1991
by Virginia Miller
First published in Great
Britain in 1991 by
Walker Books Ltd.
First published in the
United States in 1991
by Greenwillow Books.

recording, or by any information
storage and retrieval system,
without permission in writing
from the Publisher, Greenwillow
Books, a division of William Morrow
& Company, Inc., 1350 Avenue of
the Americas, New York, NY 10019.

Printed in Hong Kong by South
China Printing Company (1988) Ltd.

First American Edition

10 9 8 7 6 5 4 3 2 1

Library of Congress
Cataloging-in-Publication Data
Miller, Virginia.
On your potty / by Virginia Miller.
p.   cm.
Summary: Young bear Bartholomew finds that
using his potty correctly is sometimes just
a matter of the right timing.
ISBN 0-688-10617-X (trade).
ISBN 0-688-10618-8 (lib. bdg.)
[1. Toilet training—Fiction.
2. Bears—Fiction.]   I. Title.
PZ7.M6373On   1991
[E]—dc20   90-49221   CIP   AC

One morning George padded quietly over to
Bartholomew's bed to see if he was awake.
He asked softly, "Are you awake, Ba?"

"Nah!" said Bartholomew.

George asked, "Are you up, Ba?"

"Nah!" said Bartholomew.

George asked,

"Do you need your potty, Ba?"

"Nah!" said Bartholomew.

"Nah,   nah,

nah, nah, NAH!" said Bartholomew.

"On your

potty!"

George said
in a big voice.

Bartholomew

sat on his potty.

He tried …

and he tried …   **but nothing happened.**

"Nah!" said Bartholomew

in a little voice.

"Never mind," said George.

"Out you go and play, and be good."

"Nah!" said Bartholomew,
and off he went.

Suddenly Bartholomew thought,

On your potty!

He ran …

and he ran …

as fast as he could …

and reached his potty ...

just … in … time.

He padded proudly off to find George,

who gave him a great big hug.

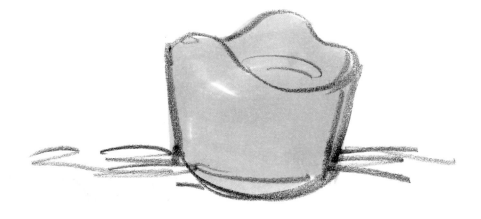